Coyote the Fire Thief

by Mick Gowar and James Rey Sanchez

TTS

Coyote the Fire Thief

Contents

Chapter 1

When Animals Ruled

Long ago, when the Earth was young, animals, not people, ruled the world. Manitou, the Great Creator Spirit, had given the animals all they needed to rule the lakes, the mountains and the forests.

He had given Squirrel and Chipmunk supple bodies that weighed barely as much as a breath of wind so they could climb tall trees and scamper along the thinnest branches to eat the sweetest fruits and tastiest nuts. He had given Coyote speed and strength, sharp teeth and strong claws so she could hunt and kill her food.

All the animals felt sorry for the poor humans. Humans were weak and clumsy, they had no sharp claws to catch and kill food and no thick fur to keep them warm during the icicle-sharp winter nights.

Humans were shy, timid creatures who crept about beneath the trees in the forest, hiding from Coyote and the other animals with sharp teeth and claws.

All the humans had to eat were the fruit and nuts that Squirrel and Chipmunk dropped and the bitter leaves and tough roots that no animal wanted to eat.

At this time, humans didn't know how to make
fire, so they couldn't cook their food, or make
pots, or forge tools of metal.

And when winter came, while Coyote, Squirrel
and Chipmunk were snug and warm in their fur,
the poor humans shivered and shook, coughed
and sneezed, until the snow and ice melted
in the spring.

Coyote was proud and clever, but she was also
kind. She watched the humans shivering and
shaking, coughing and sneezing.

"Poor things," she thought. "They don't have
thick fur to keep them warm like me.
They don't have snug burrows to keep them
warm like Squirrel and Chipmunk. I'm so lucky,
and I should help them. But how?"

Chapter 2

Coyote's Idea

Coyote walked to the edge of the forest. She sat down on a hollow log under the snow-covered branches of a great ash tree and thought.

She gazed across the flat prairie lands to the far mountains and thought. She sang a sorrowful song to herself of how sad she felt for the humans.

Then, as she sang, she noticed a red and orange glow on top of the great hollow mountain in the far distance, and she had an idea ...

"I know how I can help the humans," said Coyote. "I'll take some fire from the Fire Beings who live on top of the hollow mountain and I'll give it to the humans. Fire will keep them warm in the winter."

Coyote lifted her head and sang the great summoning song to call the other creatures to her.

Squirrel and Chipmunk heard Coyote's song

and ran as fast as they could to meet her.

"What's wrong, Coyote?" asked Squirrel.

"Are you hurt?" said Chipmunk.

"I'm going to do something very dangerous,"

said Coyote. "I need your help. Listen ..."

Chapter 3

The Fire Beings

The Fire Beings sat gazing at the great bubbling pool of boiling liquid fire at the top of the hollow mountain. Their faces glowed, and their orange hair flickered like flames in the wind.

As Coyote crept towards them, the largest
of the Fire Beings leapt to his feet.

"Who's there?" he roared. "I can hear someone
moving in the darkness. Answer me, who are you?"

"It's only me," said Coyote, in her smallest voice.
"Just a coyote. You've nothing to fear, I can't hurt
powerful beings like you."

"What do you want, Coyote?" asked the Fire Being
suspiciously. He glared at the cowering Coyote.

"I only want to warm myself for a moment or two by your fire," replied Coyote in a shaky, shivery voice. "It's a very cold night; the snow is falling and the ponds and lakes are all frozen. Please, let me sit by your fire to warm myself."

She sidled around the Fire Being's glowing leg and crept a little closer to the fire.

"Oh my! The snow must have crept under my fur and into my bones," said Coyote in a quivery, quavery voice. "Please let me move a little closer to your fire – you've nothing to fear from me."

Coyote crept even closer to the fire.

"Your fire is so beautiful," said Coyote in an admiring, adoring voice, "almost as beautiful as you, Fire Beings."

The largest of the Fire Beings glowed even brighter with pride and ran his burning hands over his blazing hair.

"Let me move a little closer to your fire to worship it – and to worship you!"

Coyote crept still closer to the fire.

"It's oh so very beautiful!" said Coyote in an amazed and awestruck voice.

Quickly, she grabbed a piece of fire.

Then, she turned and ran, leaping away from

the Fire Beings as as fast as she could.

Chapter 4

Stolen

"Stop!" cried the Fire Beings. "Come back, you scoundrel! Come back, you thief!"

They ran after Coyote, faster than flames can sweep through dry leaves in a forest.

Coyote skittered and slithered down the steep side of the hollow mountain, but the Fire Beings ran faster than molten lava can flow down a mountainside.

The largest of the Fire Beings
caught up with Coyote and tried
to seize her beautiful grey-brown
tail. At the touch of the Fire Being,
the tip of Coyote's tail burnt black
(and so it remains to this very day).

"Help! My friends, where are you?" cried Coyote.

"Here I am," called Squirrel. "Throw the fire to me!"

Squirrel caught the fire on her back and fled down

the mountainside. But within moments,

her fur was smouldering.

"Help me!" cried Squirrel, desperately. "The fire –

it's burning me!" Her back was scorched black,

and the pain had made her long tail curl up into

a tight ball (and so it remains to this very day).

"I'm here," called Chipmunk. "Quick! Pass it to me!" She seized the fire and scampered towards the forest.

Chipmunk ran as fast as she could, but the Fire Beings ran even faster. Chipmunk reached the hollow log at the edge of the forest, but the Fire Beings were already there – waiting.

"Give us back our fire!" shouted the Fire Beings.
But brave Chipmunk scrambled into the hollow
log, carrying the fire.

"Return our stolen fire!" howled the Fire Beings.
But brave Chipmunk only scurried deeper and
deeper into the hollow log.

"We demand our fire NOW!"
screamed the Fire Beings.

But brave Chipmunk pushed the fire deep into the hollow log, burying the soul of the fire deep in the heart of the wood.

"Got you!" shouted the largest of the Fire Beings. He tried to grab Chipmunk with his flaming claws. Chipmunk was too quick for him, but the red-hot claws of the Fire Being burnt three stripes down her back (which remain there to this very day).

Chapter 5

The Gift

Brave Chipmunk and Squirrel
showed the humans where
the fire was hidden, deep in
the heart of the wood.
Clever Coyote taught
the humans to break off dry sticks and rub them
together to release the fire from out of the wood
where plucky Chipmunk had hidden it.

And were the humans grateful?
No, they were not.

They used the fire to smelt iron to make axes and ploughs. They cut down the forest where Squirrel and Chipmunk and their children lived, and ploughed up the flat prairie lands where Coyote and her children lived.

They turned the land into farms, and they called Coyote, Squirrel and Chipmunk 'pests' and 'vermin'.

They used the fire to smelt iron and they made sharp-fanged traps, and they made spears and arrows, guns and bullets to catch and kill Coyote, Squirrel and Chipmunk.

Then the humans kept warm in the winter by making coats from animals' fur. They even hung the animal heads on the walls of their lodges and cabins as hunting trophies.

So now Coyote, Squirrel and Chipmunk hide in fear from the humans they once helped.

And now when Coyote comes to the edge of the forest and sings into the night, she sings a sorrowful song of how she wishes she had never stolen fire for the humans.

Things to think about

1. What sort of story is this? What does it try to explain?
2. Why do you think that Coyote and her friends put themselves in danger to help the humans?
3. What physical characteristics are the animals left with?
4. What kind of friend is Coyote?
5. In this retelling of the traditional tale, the author has considered the negative consequences of humans having fire. Do you agree with his opinion? Why or why not?

Write it yourself

This story is based on a Native American traditional tale which seeks to explain how something came to be. Now try to write your own story with a similar aim, or write your own new twist for a traditional tale that you know. Plan your story before you begin to write it.

Start off with a story map:

• a beginning to introduce the characters and where and when your story is set (the setting);

• a problem which the main characters will need to fix in the story;

• an ending where the problems are resolved.

Get writing! In traditional tales, animals are often given human characteristics, for example, human speech and emotion. Make sure the animals in your story are developed into human-like characters.

Notes for parents and carers

Independent reading

The aim of independent reading is to read this book with ease. This series is designed to provide an opportunity for your child to read for pleasure and enjoyment. These notes are written for you to help your child make the most of this book.

About the book

In this retelling of the Native American tale, we meet the trickster Coyote who takes pity on the humans and risks her and her friends' lives to bring them fire. In so doing, she and her friends not only receive aspects of their physical appearance but, in this version, bring about human destructution of their world.

Before reading

Ask your child why they have selected this book. Look at the title and blurb together. What do they think it will be about? Do they think they will like it?

During reading

Encourage your child to read independently. If they get stuck on a longer word, remind them that they can find syllable chunks that can be sounded out from left to right. They can also read on in the sentence and think about what would make sense.

After reading

Support comprehension by talking about the story. What happened?
Then help your child think about the messages in the book that go beyond the story, using the questions on the page opposite. Give your child a chance to respond to the story, asking:
Did you enjoy the story and why? Who was your favourite character?
What was your favourite part? What did you expect to happen at the end?

Franklin Watts
First published in Great Britain in 2019
by The Watts Publishing Group

Series Editors: Jackie Hamley and Melanie Palmer
Series Advisors: Dr Sue Bodman and Glen Franklin
Series Designer: Peter Scoulding

A CIP catalogue record for this book is
available from the British Library.

ISBN 978 1 4451 6447 2 (hbk)
ISBN 978 1 4451 6448 9 (pbk)
ISBN 978 1 4451 6837 1 (library ebook)

Printed in China

Franklin Watts
An imprint of
Hachette Children's Group
Part of The Watts Publishing Group
Carmelite House
50 Victoria Embankment
London EC4Y 0DZ

An Hachette UK Company
www.hachette.co.uk

www.franklinwatts.co.uk